Cowgirl Kate and Cocoa

School Days

Cowgirl Kate and Cocoa

School Days

Written by Erica Silverman

Painted by Betsy Lewin

SCHOLASTIC INC.
New York Toronto London Auckland Sydney
Mexico City New Delhi Hong Kong Buenos Aires

To Zoe and her big sister, Julia—with love—E. S.

To Claire Rose Reilly—B. L.

ISBN-13: 978-0-545-11549-0
ISBN-10: 0-545-11549-3

12 11 10 9 8 7 6 5 4 3 2 1   8 9 10 11 12 13/0

Printed in the U.S.A.   23

First Scholastic printing, September 2008

The illustrations in this book were done in watercolors on Strathmore one-ply Bristol paper.
The display type was hand lettered by Georgia Deaver.
The text type was set in Filosophia Regular.
Designed by April Ward

Chapter 1
Mary's Lamb

Cowgirl Kate got up early.
She mucked Cocoa's stall.

She groomed him and fed him.
Then she led him to the corral.
"I'll see you later," she said.
"Where are you going?" he asked.
"I have to get ready for school,"
she said.

"You can't go to school," he said.

"You have to stay home and play with me."

"Cocoa, it's fall," said Cowgirl Kate,

"and in the fall, I go to school."

"Then take me with you," he said.

Cowgirl Kate sighed.

"I can't. Horses are not allowed at school."

Cowgirl Kate went inside
and changed her clothes.
Then she hurried to the bus stop.
"See you later, Cocoa!" she called.

"Don't leave me!" cried Cocoa.
  He banged the gate again and again
  until the fence swung open.
"Wait!" cried Cocoa,
  and he galloped after the bus.
"Look!" cried one of the children.
"There's a horse following us."
"That's not a horse," someone else said.
"That's Mary's little lamb."

Everyone laughed.
Then someone sang,
"*Mary had a little lamb,*
  little lamb, little lamb..."
Everyone joined in.
"*He followed her to school one day,*
  school one day, school one day.
  He followed her to school one day,
  which was against the rules."

The driver stopped the bus.

"Whose horse is that?" he asked.

Cowgirl Kate blushed.

She raised her hand.

"Ride your horse home," said the driver.

"I'll follow you."

Cowgirl Kate stomped over to Cocoa.
She climbed on his back.
"Giddyup home," she said.

But Cocoa did not move.
"Giddyup home," she said again.
Still he did not move.

"The children on the bus
  are calling you Mary's little lamb," she said.
"They think you are a big baby."

Cocoa snorted.
"I am not a big baby,
and I am not a little lamb."
He raised his head high.
"Hold on tight," he said.
And *ta-dum ta-dum ta-dum.*
He galloped home as fast as he could.

Cowgirl Kate put him back in the corral.
Cocoa nudged her.
"Go to school right now!" he said.
Cowgirl Kate looked puzzled.

"I thought you wanted me to stay
    here," she said.
"Now you want me to go to school. Why?"
    Cocoa grinned.
"So you can hurry up and come home."

Chapter 2
The Portrait

Cowgirl Kate came home from school.
"Snack time," said Cocoa.

Cowgirl Kate gave him an apple.
He nuzzled her pocket.
She gave him another apple.
He nuzzled her pocket again.
"Snack time is over," she said.
"Now it's time for homework."

Cowgirl Kate set up an easel.

"I have to paint a picture," she said.

"Paint a picture of me," said Cocoa.

"Will you stand still?" she asked.

"I will stand very still," he said.

And he raised his head high.

Cowgirl Kate looked at him for a long time.

She started to paint.

Cocoa smacked his lips.

"Snack time," he said.

"Not yet," she said.

"Are you sure?" he asked.

"Shh!" she said.

"Can I peek?" he asked.

"Not yet," she said.

"I can't wait," he said.

And he peeked at the picture.

"You made my tail too short," he said.

She made his tail longer.

"You made my mane too light," he said.

She made his mane darker.

"Why is my mouth open?" he asked.

"Because you were talking,"

she said.

Cocoa studied the picture.
"Do you like it?" asked Cowgirl Kate.
"Yes," he said, "but . . ."
"But what?" she asked.

"I am too thin," he said.

"I need to fatten myself up."

    And he went off to nibble sweetgrass.

Chapter 3
A New Friend

Cowgirl Kate got off the
school bus with a new friend.
"Cocoa," she said,
"I want you to meet Jenny."

Cocoa snorted.

Then he turned away.

"Cocoa, turn around," said Cowgirl Kate.

But Cocoa did not.

"Your horse does not like me," said Jenny.

"He just has to get to know you,"
said Cowgirl Kate.

Cowgirl Kate and Jenny played basketball.
"Cocoa, come play with us!"
called Cowgirl Kate.
But Cocoa did not.

Cowgirl Kate showed Jenny how to rope.
"Cocoa, come rope with us!"
called Cowgirl Kate.
But Cocoa did not.

Cowgirl Kate and Jenny had milk and cookies.

"Cocoa, come have a treat!"
called Cowgirl Kate.
Cocoa took a step closer,
but he did not join them.
"I hope he is not sick,"
said Cowgirl Kate.

Jenny's mother came to take Jenny home.
Jenny took a bag from her backpack.
"I forgot. I brought you a present," she said.

"Thank you," said Cowgirl Kate.

"See you in school."

Jenny and her mother drove away.

Cowgirl Kate hurried over to Cocoa.

"Cocoa," she asked, "are you sick?"

Cocoa sighed.

"I am heartsick," he said.

"You have school.

You have a new friend.

Soon you will forget all about me."

And he slouched away.

"Cocoa, wait!" she called.

"I have a yummy treat for you."

Cocoa stopped.

"Why would you give me a treat?" he asked.

"You don't like me anymore."

"Of course I like you," said Cowgirl Kate.

She stroked his neck.

"You are my best friend in the whole world."

"I am?" asked Cocoa.

"Yes, you are," said Cowgirl Kate.

"And nothing will ever change that."

"Not school?" he asked.

"Not school," she replied.

"Not a new friend?" he asked.

"Not a new friend," she replied.

Cocoa sighed.

Then he nudged her hand.

"I am ready for my treat now," he said.

Cowgirl Kate popped a peppermint candy
into his mouth.

"Yum!" he said.

"Where did you get such good treats?"

Cowgirl Kate smiled.

"They are a present from Jenny."

Cocoa grinned.

"I am happy we have a new friend," he said.

Chapter 4
A Report

Cowgirl Kate was in her bedroom.

Cocoa stuck his head in the window.

"Play with me," he said.

"I can't," she replied.

"I'm writing a report."

"Can you play with a report?" he asked.

"No," she said.

"Then what good is it?" he asked.

"It has a good topic," she said.

"It's about horses."

"I know about horses," he said.

"I will help you."

So Cowgirl Kate took her
notebook outside.

"Read me your report," said Cocoa.

She read, "Horses have long, graceful tails."

"That's true," said Cocoa.

And he flicked his long,
graceful tail.

"Horses have long, flowing manes,"
she read.
"That's true, too," he said.
And he tossed his long, flowing mane.

"Horses come in black, white,
   brown, tan, or gray," she read.
"Wait a minute," he said.
"I am the color of chocolate.
   My mane and tail are the color of caramel."
"You are special," she said.
"That is very true," he agreed.

"What else should I write?"
asked Cowgirl Kate.
"I will show you," said Cocoa.
He trotted and cantered.

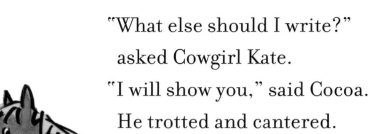

Horses like to trot and canter,
Cowgirl Kate wrote.

He galloped and jumped.
Horses like to gallop and jump,
she wrote.

He rolled on his back.

Horses like to roll on their backs, she wrote.

"And now," said Cocoa,
"can you guess what horses like to do
  most of all?"
"Eat?" she guessed.
  And she held out an apple.
  Cocoa chomped it.
"Close," he said.
"But I was thinking of something else."
"Give me a hint," she said.
  He gave her a nudge.

"Tag!" he squealed. "You're it!"
Cowgirl Kate laughed.
She wrote, *Most of all, horses*
like to play with their friends.
Then she put down her notebook
and chased Cocoa all
around the yard.